This Little Tiger book belongs to:

_____

_____

_____

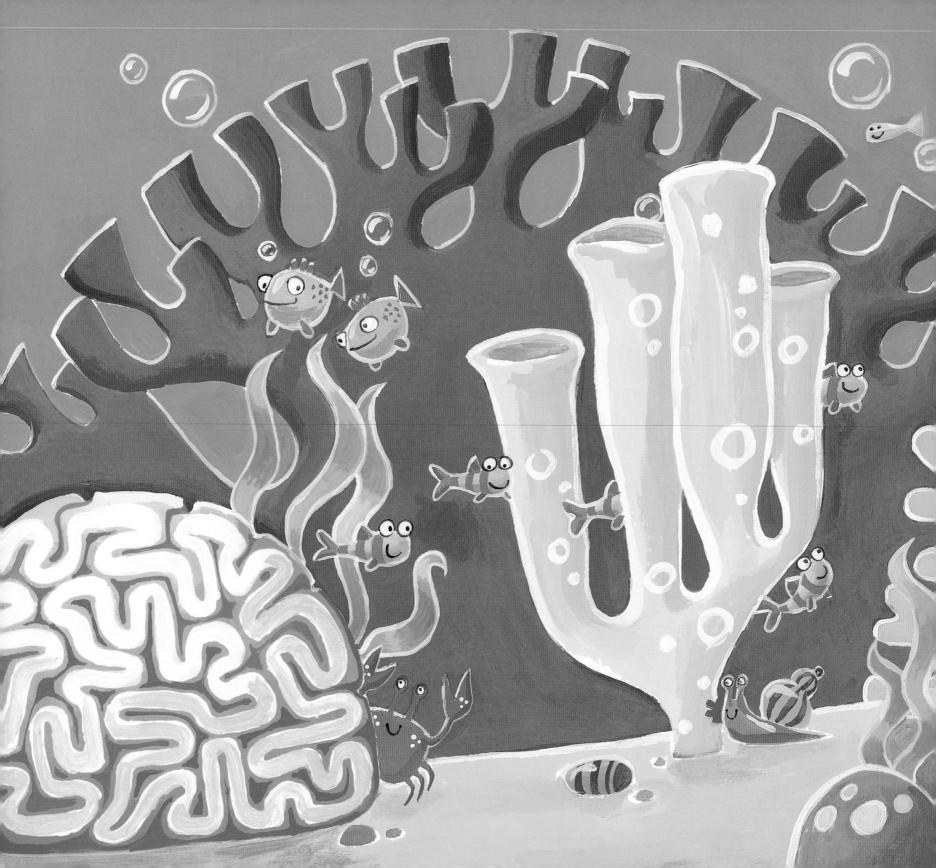

To Wayne, with love

LITTLE TIGER PRESS LTD,
an imprint of the Little Tiger Group
1 The Coda Centre, 189 Munster Road,
London SW6 6AW
www.littletiger.co.uk

First published in Great Britain 2003
This edition published 2016

Text and illustrations copyright © Ruth Galloway 2003
Ruth Galloway has asserted her right to be
identified as the author and illustrator of this work
under the Copyright, Designs and Patents Act, 1988

A CIP catalogue record for this book is available
from the British Library

Printed in China • LTP/1400/1885/0417

1 3 5 7 9 10 8 6 4 2

# Smiley Shark

Ruth Galloway

LITTLE TIGER

LONDON

Far away, in a deep rolling ocean, lived Smiley Shark . . .
the smiliest and sunniest, the friendliest and funniest,
the biggest and toothiest of all the fish.

Every day Smiley Shark watched the beautiful fish
that dipped and dived and jiggled and jived,
and darted and dashed with a splosh and a splash.

Smiley Shark longed to dip and dive
with them. But whenever he smiled at the
other fish they swam away.

"Will YOU play with me?"
he asked Angelfish.

Angelfish shivered and shook,
then raced away as fast as she could swim.

Pufferfish was blowing bubbles.
"That looks fun!" laughed Smiley Shark.
But Pufferfish blew himself up into
a big spiky ball and pricked poor
Smiley Shark on the nose!

Starfish was twirling and whirling,
dancing and prancing.
"What fun!" giggled Smiley Shark.
But Starfish cartwheeled off across the
ocean floor as far away as she could go.

SWIRL!

Smiley Shark flashed his grin at Jellyfish . . .

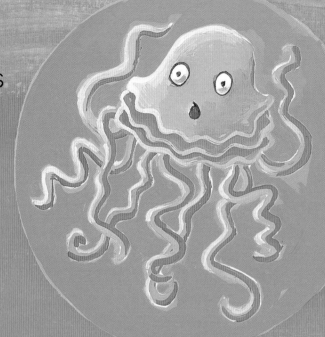

and Octopus . . .

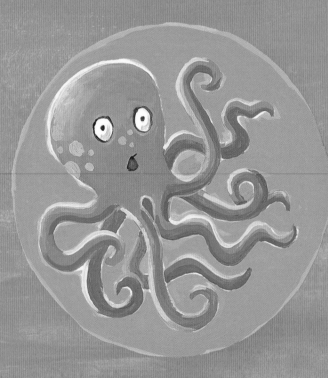

and Catfish.

Off they swam,
as far from Smiley Shark
as they could get.

"Everyone is scared of my big white teeth," wailed Smiley Shark. He didn't feel much like smiling any more.

SPLISH! SPLASH!
Twisting and turning, splashing and churning,
the fish danced faster than ever. Smiley Shark
watched from a distance. But something was wrong.
The fish were swimming towards a . . .

# ...TRAP!

"Help!" cried the fish.
"Please help us, Smiley Shark!"

Smiley Shark swam round and
round the fisherman's net.
What could he do? How could he help?
The only thing Smiley Shark could do was . . .

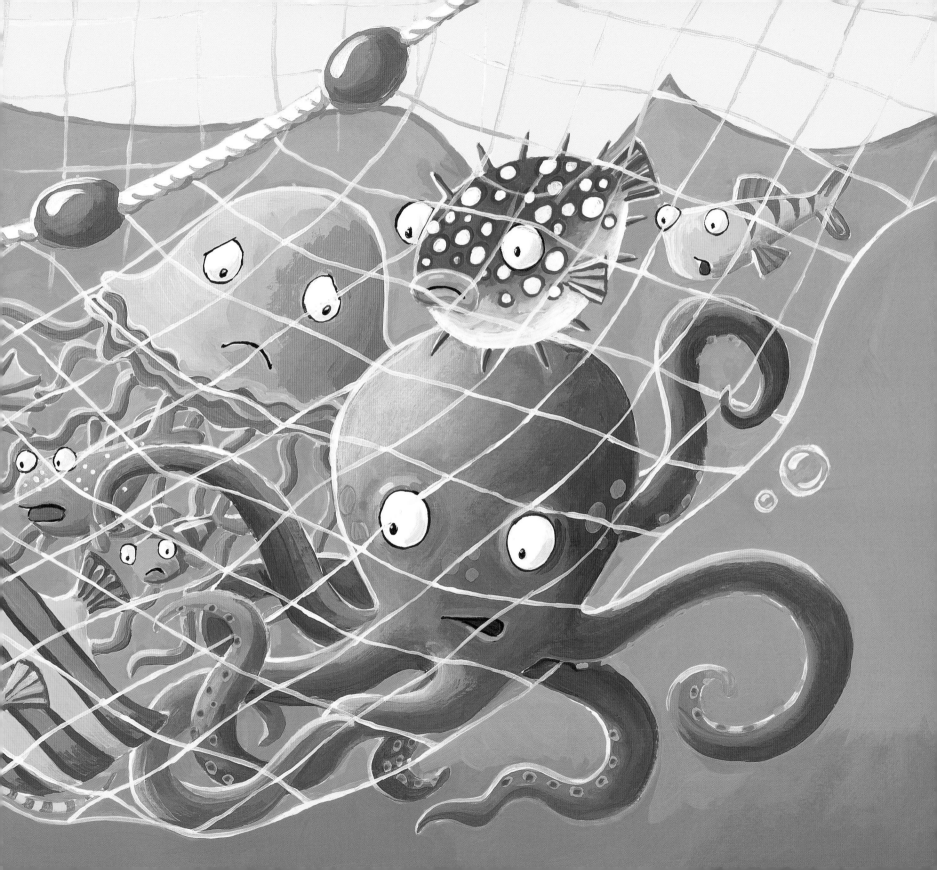

"Hurrah!" cheered the fish.
"We're safe! Thank you, Smiley Shark!"

Now far away, in the deep rolling ocean,
Smiley Shark and his friends can be seen,
dipping and diving, darting and dashing,
sploshing and splashing and

# SMILING!

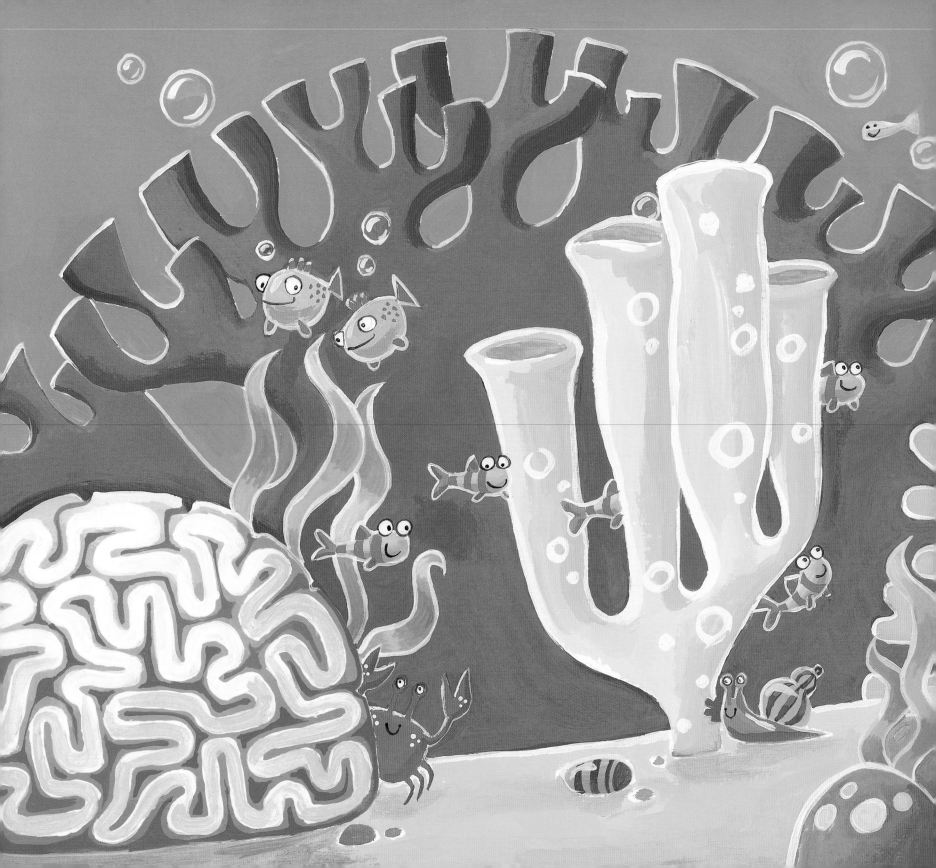

# More fabulous books from Little Tiger Press!

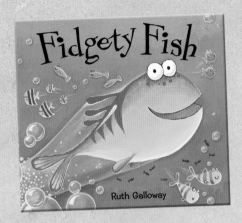

Fidgety Fish

Ruth Galloway

Gillian Lobel

Little Honey Bear and the Smiley Moon

Tim Warnes

STEVE SMALLMAN

THE LAMB WHO CAME FOR DINNER

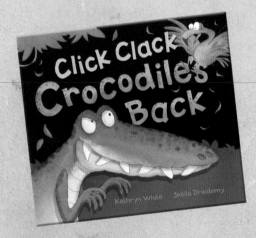

Click Clack Crocodile's Back

Kathryn White  Joëlle Dreidemy

Puppy's First Christmas

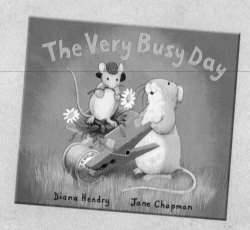

The Very Busy Day

Diana Hendry  Jane Chapman

For information regarding any of the above titles
or for our catalogue, please contact us:
Little Tiger Press, 1 The Coda Centre,
189 Munster Road, London SW6 6AW
Tel: 020 7385 6333
E-mail: contact@littletiger.co.uk
www.littletiger.co.uk

Image taken from *Little Honey Bear and the Smiley Moon* copyright © Tim Warnes 2006